THE USBORNE BOOK OF
DISGUISE

Vivien Kelly

Designed by Non Figg

Edited by Fiona Watt

Series Editor: Cheryl Evans

Illustrated by **Kevin Lyle**
Photographs by **Ray Moller** and **Howard Allman**
Face painter and make-up consultant: **Caro Childs**

Contents

Disguising yourself

Disguising yourself is great fun because you get to be anybody you like for a while. Next time you are out, notice exactly how other people look and move so that you can try to copy them later. Take time to disguise yourself properly so that you look convincing, then fool your family, trick your friends and see how it feels to be somebody else.

The basic kit

You can use ordinary make-up or face paints to disguise your face. Always test anything you are going to put on your skin first, in case you are allergic to it.

Talcum powder

Gel

Hairspray

Eye shadow

Foundation

Liquid latex (Copydex glue)

Body oil

Wool for fake hair

Eye pencil

Lipstick

Plasters

Hair grips

Cotton wool balls

Derma wax

Face paints

You can buy face paints from toy shops or fancy dress shops. The best kind to use are water-based face paints which come in single pots or in a palette.

Liquid latex

To make fake scars and warts you will need liquid latex. You can use Copydex glue which you can get in most stationery shops.

Derma wax

Derma wax is a kind of wax which you can use to make fake noses and chins. You can buy it from fancy dress shops or theatrical shops. When you use it you need to add body oil to it to stop the wax from becoming too sticky.

Fancy dress shops

There are many other things for disguise which you can buy in fancy dress shops, such as false beards, noses, scars and wigs as well as special face paints and make-up.

Secret notebook

To make your disguises look convincing, take a good look at other people's faces, hairstyles and clothes. Draw people's beards, noses or hats in a notebook so that you don't forget what they looked like. You could then try to copy them later. Look closely at how other people dress and behave but don't stare at them.

You could also make a note of how each person was walking.

Portrait gallery

These people all appear in this book. See if you can spot them. You can find out on page 32 where each one appears.

Thomas Edwards *David Edwards* *Steven Milward* *Tim Sandhu*

Daniel Turner *Rachel Wells* *Lizzie Kelly* *Nila Simon* *Elizabeth Maguire*

Emma Lee *Jake Lee* *Jo Litchfield* *Laura Wade* *Zoe Hutchinson*

Disguising your hair

Changing your hairstyle is good way to begin to diguise yourself. These pages show you to create different styles for both short and long hair. For most of them you will need to gel your hair. To do this put a little hair gel on your fingers and run them through your hair. Style your hair with a brush, a comb or your fingers. The gel comes out when you wash your hair.

You will need: a brush; a comb; hair gel. If you have long hair - a small covered band and a headband. If you don't have any gel use water instead.

This page has styles for short hair. Put some gel on your fingers and run them through your hair. Pull the top and sides up into spikes. Keep doing this until the gel dries.

Put gel on your hands and run them through your hair. Use a comb to part your hair in the middle then pull each side into a peak above your ears. Do this until the gel dries.

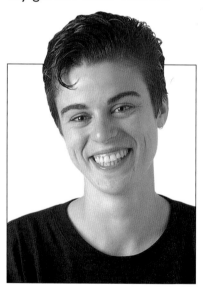

Gel all of your hair and comb it back. Comb the front and the sides of your hair up and forward. Take a little bit of hair and make a curl in the middle of your forehead.

Gel your hair and comb it all back. Use eyeliner to draw a 'V' in the middle of your forehead coming down from your hairline. Fill in the shape with upward strokes.

Gel your hair and part it in the middle. Take some hair from each side and push it up in the middle. Keep holding it up until the gel dries. Brush the rest of your hair back.

These are styles for long hair. Gather some of your hair into a very high ponytail. Put some gel on the ends of the ponytail and brush them down over your forehead and face.

If you want to disguise yourself as a man, gel your hair and brush it back. Part it in the middle then fasten it at the top of your neck. Tuck the ponytail into your clothes.

Gel your hair then part it at one side just above your ear. Tie a loose ponytail at your neck then brush your hair over your head. Hide the ponytail under a hat.

To look as if you have short hair, put on a headband and push it back behind your ears. Gel your hair and brush it forward over the headband like a fringe. Put a hat on top.

Bend over and fasten all your hair into a ponytail on top of your head. Stand up and gel the hair. Separate the ponytail in two then plait each piece. Hide the ponytail under a hat.

Brush your hair well. Put a headband on and push it far back behind your ears. Put some gel on your hair and brush some of your hair forward over the headband.

Fake hair

You will need: wool that matches your hair; scissors. **For the bun:** sponge; hairnet that matches your hair; tape; elastic band; headband; covered bands; hair gel; hair grips. **For the plait:** two covered bands; hairgrips; gel. **For the bald head:** white rubber swimming cap; household glue (PVA); piece of cardboard; face paint; foundation.

Put on a headband to hide the edge of the hairnet.

Fake bun

Don't wind the wool too tightly around the sponge.

Fasten it with an elastic band.

1. Cut the sponge into a ball slightly smaller than you want your bun. Tape wool to the sponge and wind it around.

2. Cover the sponge then cut and tie the end of the wool. Fasten the sponge in the middle of the hairnet.

3. Gel or tie your hair back. Put the hairnet on your head. Fasten the bun in place with some hair grips.

Fake plait

Use an elastic band to fasten the wool.

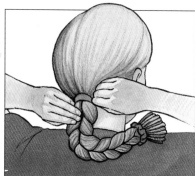

1. Cut thirty strands of wool slightly longer than you want the plait to be. Fasten them together at one end.

2. Put the fastened end under a heavy book on the edge of a table. Separate the wool into three parts and plait it.

3. Fasten the end with a covered band. Tie or gel back your hair. Attach the plait to your head with hair grips.

Hide the end of a fake plait under a hat.

Face paint some wrinkles on your forehead.

Bald head

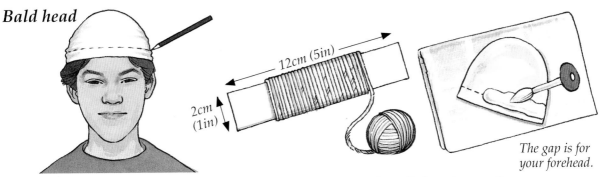

The gap is for your forehead.

1. Pull a swimming cap down tightly on your head. Draw a line in pencil around the cap, 5cm (2in) from the bottom.

2. Cut a piece of cardboard 2 x 12cm (1 x 5in). Cut about 3m (10ft) of wool and wind it around the cardboard.

3. Lay the cap flat on some newspaper. Put glue along the pencil line but leave a 4cm (2in) gap at the left end.

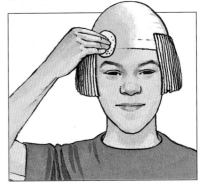

4. Cut the wool along the long edge of the card. Press half of the wool onto the glue so it hangs down like hair.

5. Turn the cap over. Spread on glue and press the rest of the wool on this side. Leave a gap on the right this time.

6. Put the cap on and cover over all the white rubber with foundation. Try to blend the join in with your skin.

Moustaches

To disguise yourself as a man, try wearing a fake moustache.

You will need, for a wool moustache: wool; a plaster or plaster strip; household glue (PVA); scissors; a pencil.
For a cotton wool moustache: a small plaster; thread; cotton wool balls; scissors; household glue (PVA).
For a painted moustache: face paints or black eyeliner.

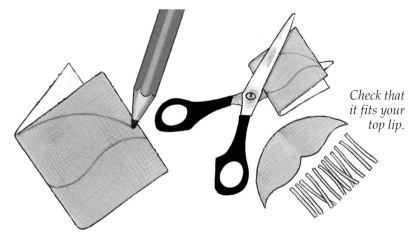

Check that it fits your top lip.

Wear a moustache which suits your disguise.

1. Fold a plaster in half. Use a pencil to draw half of a moustache shape along the fold, like this.

2. Cut it out through both layers of the plaster and then lay it flat. Cut some wool into pieces 2cm (1in) long.

Overlap the top and bottom layers of wool.

3. Brush a line of glue along the front of the plaster, near to the bottom. Press some of the pieces of wool onto it.

4. When the glue is dry, put another line of glue along the top of the plaster. Press another row of wool along it.

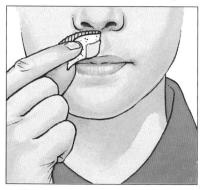

5. When the glue is dry, trim the wool so it looks tidy. Peel the backing off the plaster and press it above your top lip.

6. When you want to remove the moustache, peel it off gently, as you would with an ordinary plaster.

Cotton wool moustache

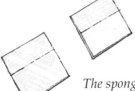

The sponge makes it easier for you to pull the moustache off.

Glue on the squares with the sponge at the bottom.

1. Unroll a cotton ball and carefully cut it to the size and shape you want it. Tie a piece of thread around its middle.

2. Cut out two small squares of plaster making sure that each has a piece of sponge backing on it.

3. Glue these to the back of each side of the moustache. Unpeel the plastic backing and press them onto your face.

Whiskers

Trim the wool so that it looks neat.

1. Stand in front of a mirror and hold a plaster strip under your nose. Draw the shape of a moustache onto the strip.

2. Cut the shape out. Cut the wool into 2cm (1in) pieces and follow steps 3,4 and 5 of the wool moustache instructions.

Painted moustache

1. Make sure that your mouth is relaxed and you are not smiling. Find an eyeliner which matches your hair.

2. Draw an outline of the moustache shape you want above your top lip. Shade it in with downward strokes.

Beards and stubble

You will need: household glue (PVA); scissors.
For stubble: black or brown face paint or eyeliner; old toothbrush.
For beard and eyebrows: cotton wool balls; four pipecleaners; poster paint; medium-sized plaster.
For goatee beard: large plaster; wool for hair.

Fake beard and eyebrows with a bald head (page 7).

Stubbly chin

Cotton wool beard

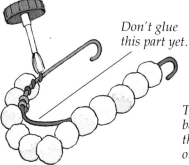

Twist the ends to join the pipecleaners.

This part will be above your mouth.

Don't glue this part yet.

To make the beard longer, glue the balls onto each other at the bottom.

1. Join three of the pipecleaners into a big U-shape. Add the fourth one onto the bottom, like this.

2. Bend the ends to hook over your ears. Put glue along the pipecleaners and press on lots of cotton wool balls.

3. Gently pull a cotton ball apart and glue a thin layer along the pipecleaner which will go above your mouth.

Cotton wool eyebrows

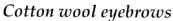

The plaster should have some sponge on it.

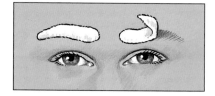

4. Once the glue is dry, brush the beard lightly. Do this carefully so that you don't break up the beard.

1. Unroll a cotton ball. Cut it into two eyebrow shapes, big enough to cover your own. Cut out two pieces of plaster.

2. Glue the non-sticky side of the plasters to each eyebrow shape. Peel off the backing and press over your eyebrow.

Goatee beard

You can buy a fake beard in a joke shop.

This beard is wool glued to a plaster, like the goatee, then plaited.

Stubble

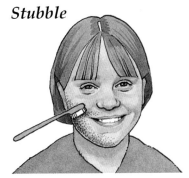

Wet a toothbrush and either rub it in face paint, or rub an eyeliner over the bristles. Dab it all over your chin.

Tip

To make a dark cotton wool beard, mix runny poster paint in a margarine tub. Dip the beard into it then lay it on newspaper to dry.

Wool goatee beard

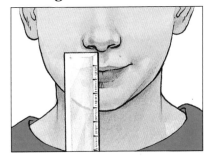

1. Use a ruler to measure the distance between the bottom of your nose and the end of your chin.

3. Draw a hole large enough for your mouth and carefully cut around it. Cut wool into 2cm (1in) pieces.

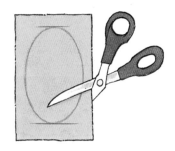

2. With a pencil, mark the distance on a large plaster. Draw an oval between the marks and cut it out.

Pull the backing paper off the plaster and press it on.

4. Turn to page 8 and follow steps 3, 4 and 5 for making a wool moustache. Press the beard on around your mouth.

11

Changing the shape of your face

You can change the shape of your face by highlighting and shading different areas. You can use face paint or eyeliner to do this (see right).

You will need: face paints; make-up sponge, **or** all of the following: foundation; lipstick; brown or black eyeliner; white eyeliner. **For hiding eyebrows:** Derma wax (see page 2); metal teaspoon; face powder.

Remember not to lick your lips when you have foundation on them.

1. Put a blob of foundation on the back of your hand. Dip your fingers into it and rub it all over your face so that it looks smooth and even.

2. Cover over your lips and eyebrows with foundation too. If you have dark eyebrows you might need to go over them again.

This makes your eyes look bigger.

This makes your chin look pointy.

3. Use lipstick or face paint, to draw new lips that are different from your own. Draw some new eyebrows with brown or black eyeliner, or face paint.

4. With eyeliner or face paint, gently draw a line under each eye, close to your lower eyelashes. Be careful not to touch your eye.

5. Shade from the edge of your jaw to under your chin. Shade up to the corners of your mouth. Highlight below your mouth (see right).

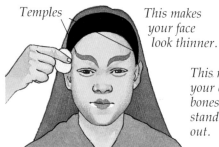

Temples

This makes your face look thinner.

This makes your cheek bones stand out.

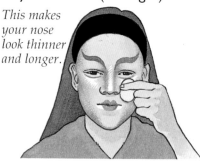

This makes your nose look thinner and longer.

6. Use a sponge to shade down both sides of your face, starting at your temples and finishing at your jaw. Shade all the way back to your hairline.

7. Press your cheeks and feel where your cheek bones are. Shade under these bones until you are 2cm (1in) from the side of your nose.

8. Highlight down your nose from between your eyebrows to the tip then highlight your cheek bones too. Shade down the sides of your nose.

Shading with eyeliner

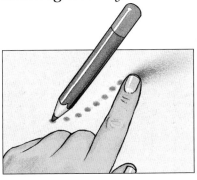

With a brown eyeliner, put dots over the area that you want to shade. Gently rub the dots with a finger so that the area looks dark and even.

Shading with face paint

Use a dark tone for shading.

Wet a make-up sponge and squeeze it so it is just damp. Rub it gently in brown face paint. Dab it lightly over the area you want to shade.

Highlighting

Use a light colour for highlighting.

To highlight with make-up or face paint do the same as you would for shading but use either white eyeliner or some white face paint.

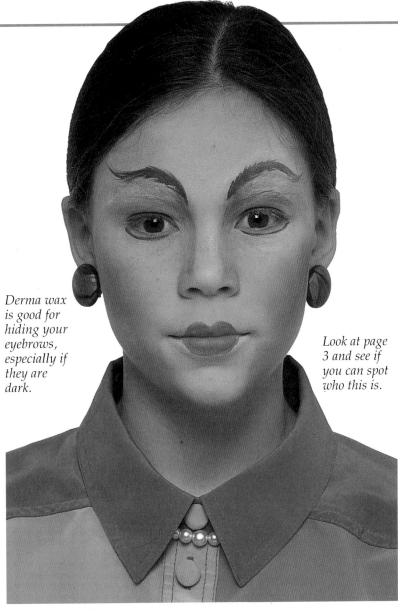

Derma wax is good for hiding your eyebrows, especially if they are dark.

Look at page 3 and see if you can spot who this is.

Hiding eyebrows

1. Warm a little Derma wax in your hands. Use the handle of a metal teaspoon to smear half of the wax carefully over one of your eyebrows.

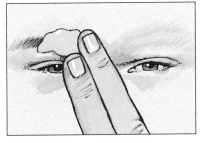

2. Do the same with the other eyebrow. Cover both patches of wax with baby oil and smooth the edges. Dust the wax with face powder.

13

Noses and chins

Changing the shape of your nose and chin makes you look very different. You can buy fake features from fancy dress shops, joke shops or theatrical suppliers, or make your own.

You will need: to change the shape of your features: playdough and foundation, **or** Derma wax (see page 2); body oil and face powder.
To make a wart: liquid latex (see page 2); a medium-sized plaster; scissors; foundation.

Derma wax noses and chins

Leave holes for your nostrils.

Sponge

1. Warm some Derma wax in your hands. Add oil if it gets sticky. Smear the Derma wax over your nose or chin.

2. Push the wax into the shape you want. Rub oil all over the wax, then put face powder over the oil.

Playdough noses

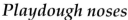

Look at the shapes below if you need a few ideas.

1. Wash your face and dry it very well. Take a piece of playdough and squash it with your hands into a thin layer.

2. Place the layer of playdough on your nose and gently smooth the edges into your face, leaving your nostrils free.

3. Gently mould the playdough into the shape you want. Cover over the playdough with foundation.

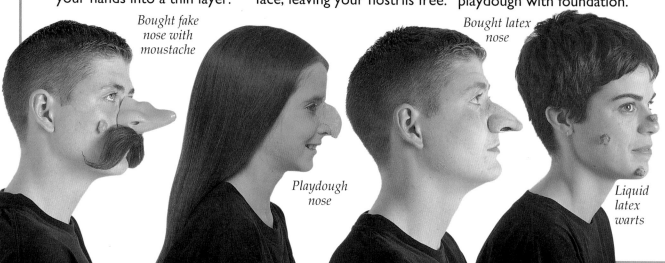

Bought fake nose with moustache

Playdough nose

Bought latex nose

Liquid latex warts

Playdough chins

Use a shade of playdough that most closely matches your skin.

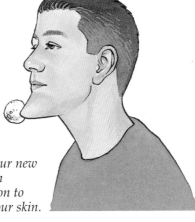

Glue the non-sticky side.

Cover your new chin with foundation to match your skin.

1. Roll a piece of playdough into a ball. Press it against your chin and mould it into the shape you want.

2. Remove the playdough and leave it to dry out. When dry, glue four plaster pieces into the dip made by your chin.

3. When the glue is dry, remove the backing from the plasters and press it on. Fill in any cracks with playdough.

Making a wart

Make sure the square of plaster has a section of sponge backing on it.

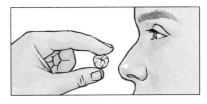

1. Paint a 2cm (1in) square of liquid latex (see page 2) on the bottom of a margarine tub. Wait for it to dry.

2. Peel the latex up around the edges and then roll it in from each side so that you get a lump of latex.

3. Glue the lump to a small square of plaster. Peel the backing paper off and press it to your skin.

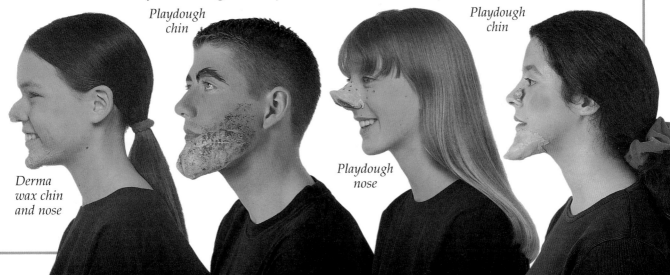

Derma wax chin and nose

Playdough chin

Playdough nose

Playdough chin

Looking old

You can change your appearance enormously by making your face and hands look old. Use make-up or face paint to make them look pale and wrinkly.

You will need: foundation; brown eyeliner; white eyeliner; red lipstick (or a box of face paints instead of all three); talcum powder; a towel. To make foundation from face paint see page 32.

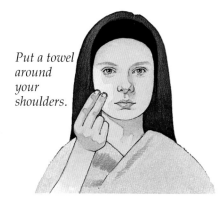

Put a towel around your shoulders.

1. Put a blob of foundation on the back of your hand. Dip your fingers into it and rub it all over your face so that it looks smooth and even.

2. Close one eye. With brown eyeliner or face paint, carefully shade from the middle of your eyelid towards your nose. Do the same for the other eye.

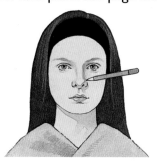

Draw in the frown lines.

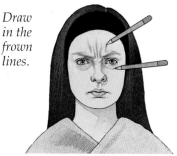

3. Gently draw a straight line from your eyebrow down each side of your nose. Stop the line when you get to your nostrils.

4. Frown in a mirror and draw in brown vertical lines on your forehead. Draw a half-circle under each eye and shade it in carefully.

5. Raise your eyebrows as high as you can. Draw along the lines on your forehead. Put an upside-down 'V' at each corner of your mouth.

If you use face paint you don't need to blend the lines in.

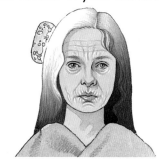

6. Make a big smile and draw in the lines around your mouth. Draw a half-circle in the dip of your chin. Put vertical lines above and below your lips.

7. With the white eyeliner or face paint put white lines on both sides of all the dark ones. Rub your finger along all the lines so they blend in.

8. Sprinkle talcum powder in your hair to make it grey. Or, wet a sponge and rub it in white face paint. Wipe it over your hair.

Hands

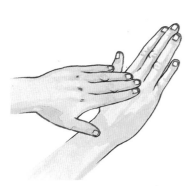 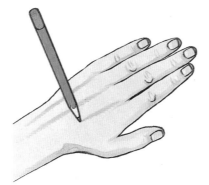 

1. Stretch out all your fingers on one hand. Rub foundation into the back of your hand and along your fingers. Repeat for your other hand.

2. Draw lines between your fingers back to your wrist with brown eyeliner or face paint. Add a line between your first finger and thumb.

3. Highlight the area between the lines with white eyeliner. Use lipstick or face paint to put some red lines on your finger joints and knuckles.

A towel over your shoulders protects your clothes from face paint or make-up.

Add some lipstick if you are disguised as an old woman.

Add some accessories that suit the disguise.

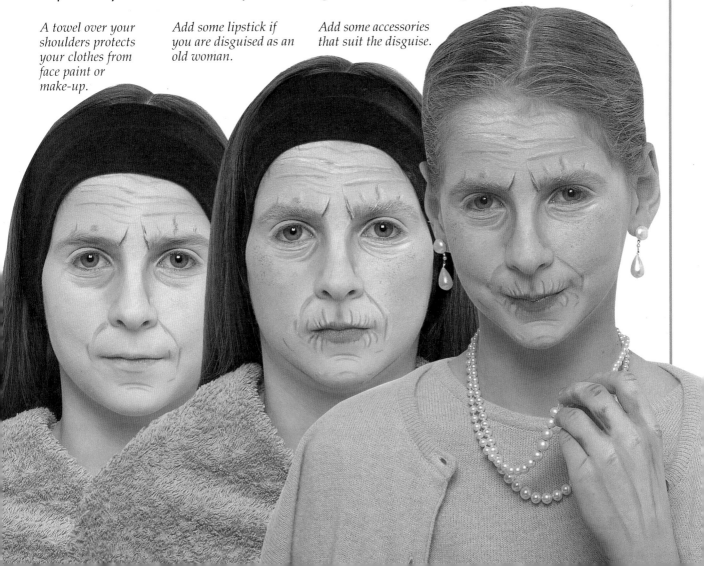

Cuts, a black eye and tattoos

You will need, for a scar: dark eyeliner or face paints. **To make a nasty cut:** liquid latex (see page 2); black thread; a medium-sized plaster; foundation; red food dye. **For a black eye:** blue, grey, and mauve eye shadow, brush. **For the tattoos:** face paints; small sponge; craft knife; ballpoint pen; masking tape; clear book-covering film.

Scar

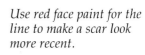

Highlight a strip on your hand (see page 13). Draw a line over it with the eyeliner. Put a row of dots on each side.

Use red face paint for the line to make a scar look more recent.

A nasty cut

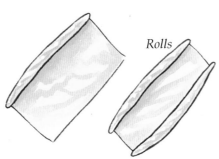

Rolls

1. Brush a square of liquid latex on the back of your hand. Let it dry. Peel up the long edges of the latex and roll them in.

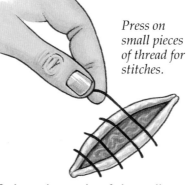

Press on small pieces of thread for stitches.

2. Join the ends of the rolls then brush food dye between them. Add another layer of latex and pieces of thread.

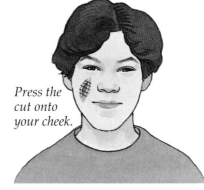

Press the cut onto your cheek.

3. To attach a fake cut to your face, when it's dry, peel it off your hand and glue it to a plaster. Peel off the backing.

Dab the edges with foundation to blend the cut into your skin.

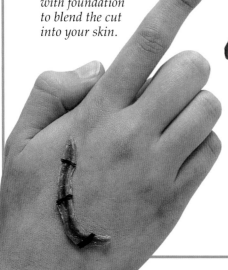

Black eye

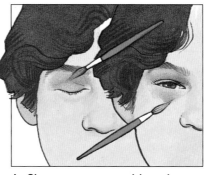

1. Shut one eye and brush blue eye shadow over the lid. Open your eye and brush the eye shadow under it too.

2. With the brush, dab other eye shadows over the blue. Make some parts around the eye darker than other parts.

Pretend tattoos

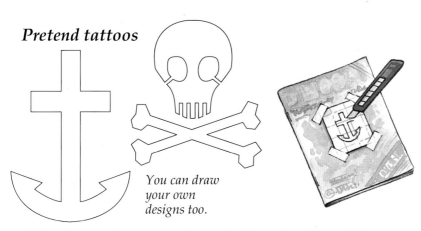

You can draw your own designs too.

1. Put the book-covering film, plastic-side down, on one of the designs above, and trace it. Leave the backing on the film.

2. Tape the piece of film onto an old magazine. Use a craft knife to cut carefully around the outline of the design.

3. Wet a small sponge with cold water. Squeeze it hard so that you get out as much water as possible.

Remember not to touch your eye - it's supposed to hurt!

Add freckles with a black or brown eye pencil.

When you want to remove the tattoos, wash them off with soap and water.

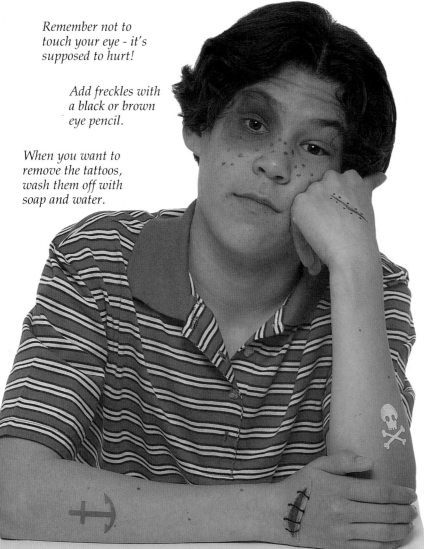

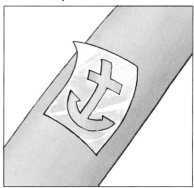

4. Carefully peel the backing paper off the film. Press the film onto a patch of clean, dry skin. Smooth it down all over.

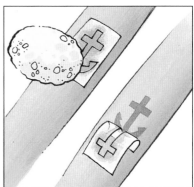

5. Rub one side of the sponge in the face paint. Dab it over the design. Let the face paint dry and peel off the film.

19

Rubber hands

You will need: rubber gloves, turned inside out; scissors; household glue (PVA).
For hanging finger: liquid latex (see page 2); playdough; margarine tub; red felt-tip pen.
For fake nails: cardboard; felt-tip pens; clear book-covering film.
For ring: kitchen foil.
For bracelet: sequins.

Cut five cardboard ovals to look like nails. Glue them onto the glove.

Glue on hairs from an old paintbrush for a hairy hand.

Hanging finger

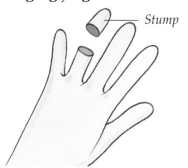

Stump

Hold the pieces until the glue is dry.

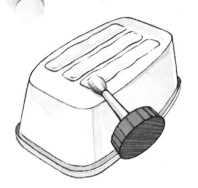

1. Cut a finger off a rubber glove, half way down. Push playdough into the cut ends, making them flat on top.

2. Brush liquid latex over the playdough in the cut finger and the stump. Brush it down the sides too.

3. Brush three strips of the latex 7cm (3in) long onto the bottom of a margarine tub. Leave them to dry.

Leave a loose end.

Cover the glove with foundation to make it look like your skin.

4. Cover the strips with red felt-tip pen. Let them dry. Peel up a long edge and roll it over and over to make a thin strip.

5. Wrap one strip around the loose finger and leave a piece sticking out. Wrap the second strip around the stump.

6. Glue the third strip to the loose finger and then to the stump. Shade in the ends of the finger with a red pen.

Fake nails

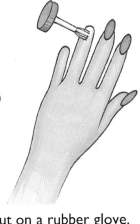

1. Cut out a piece of cardboard 15 x 8cm (6 x 3in) and colour one side of it with a bright felt-tip pen.

2. Cover the side you have coloured with clear book-covering film. Cut out ten fingernail shapes.

3. Put on a rubber glove. Glue the tops of the fingers and press on the cardboard fingernails. Let the glue dry.

Fake ring

Cover the glove with foundation to make it look more like your skin.

Make a snake bracelet in the same way as you make a ring. Start with a bigger piece of foil.

1. Cut a strip of kitchen foil 25 x 10cm (10 x 4in). Scrunch it into a thin strip. Squash one end flat and glue on a sequin.

Sequin bracelet

1. Lay the glove flat on some newspaper. Put a band of glue along the bottom. Stick several rows of sequins onto it.

Glue sequins up to the edge of the glove to disguise it.

2. With the glove on, wind the foil around your finger into a snake shape.

21

Glasses

People can easily recognize you by your eyes. Glasses, especially dark ones, help to hide them. You can also pretend to look one way when really looking the other when you wear sunglasses.

You will need: sunglasses; cardboard; paints; sequins; household glue (PVA); scissors.

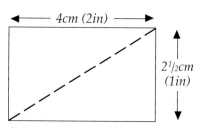

If your glasses are too big, wrap a rubber band around each stem.

1. Carefully push out the plastic lenses from a pair of sunglasses. You could just wear the frames like this.

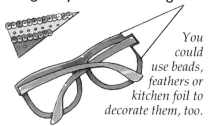

4cm (2in)

2½cm (1in)

2. To make crazy frames, cut a cardboard rectangle 2½ x 4cm (1 x 2in). Cut it diagonally into two triangles.

Make sure your outfit looks right with the glasses.

These glasses would help you disguise yourself as a bright, extravert character. You wouldn't wear them if you didn't want to be noticed!

You could use beads, feathers or kitchen foil to decorate them, too.

3. Decorate the triangles with paint and sequins. Trim the ends of the triangles to fit your frames. Glue them on.

Glasses as a prop

The way you wear or hold glasses helps your disguise.

Tie them to a long string to hang around your neck. Take them off and fiddle with them.

Push your glasses up onto the front of your head. If you have long hair, they will hold it back.

With one hand, push your glasses down to the end of your nose and peer over them, to look severe.

Scarves

Scarves can make you look scruffy or smart depending on how you wear them.

Folding a scarf

The most useful scarf is a large cotton or silky square. All the ways of tying a scarf shown on this page are done with a square scarf, folded as shown on the right.

Folded edge

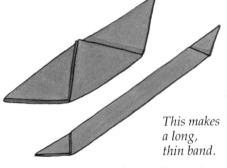

This makes a long, thin band.

1. For most basic styles, you need to take your square scarf and fold it diagonally so two opposite corners meet.

2. For variety, bring the point opposite the fold up to meet the fold, then turn the same side up again and again.

Scarf styles

Wear it around your neck.

With the fold at the top, tie the corner points at the back of your neck.

This is a good 'old lady' style

Put the folded edge against your forehead. Tie the narrow ends under your chin.

This style hides your hair well.

Have the fold on your forehead. Tie the corner points at the back, over the third point.

Here's a sporty look.

Make a band as in steps 1 and 2 above. Tie it around your forehead.

For this style put the folded edge against the back of your neck and tie the narrow ends on top of your forehead. Tuck the third point under the narrow ends at the front.

You could add some curlers under your scarf.

This girl's fringe shows, but you can completely hide your hair with a scarf; or wear fake hair poking out from under it.

Hats

Hats are great for disguising yourself because they hide your hair and some of your face too. Here are some ideas for different ways of wearing hats, adding fake hair to a hat and what to do if a hat doesn't fit.

You will need: to make hats fit: one or two pairs of socks; tape; hat. **To make fake hair:** wool; magazine; tape; scissors; old hat.

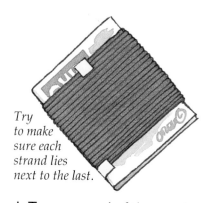

Try to make sure each strand lies next to the last.

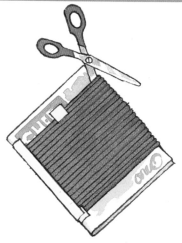

1. Tape one end of the wool to the spine of a magazine. Wind the wool around the magazine twenty times and tape the other end to the magazine too.

2. Press tape along the spine of the magazine on top of the wool. Put one blade of the scissors inside the magazine pages. Cut through the wool.

3. Put a piece of tape on the other side of the wool, in the same place as the piece you put on the spine.

4. Carefully cut through the wool along the middle of the tape. This leaves you with two hair pieces.

5. Tape each hair piece to the inside of your hat. Make sure you leave a gap in the front for your face.

Hide your face in the shadow of a hat.

Find a hat to suit your character.

Tape wool hair to a hat.

Pin the brim up with a brooch.

Ribbons

Cover with badges

Fake hair

Scarves and hat pins

Fake flowers and fruit

Accessories

There are all sorts of things you can do to a hat to make it look different. Try turning the brim up, or down; or wear it back-to-front or sideways. Add things to the hat to change its appearance: tie a scarf around it, cover it in badges or add fake fruit or feathers. You can see some of these ideas in the pictures above.

Making hats fit

1. For this you will need one or two pairs of socks. Fold the first pair of socks in half lengthways.

2. Tape each sock around the inside of your hat. Try it on for size. If it still doesn't fit add another pair of socks.

Try and find a hat that matches your outfit.

Hide your own hair under a hat.

Pulling a face

People's expressions are part of their appearance, so try to change your expression to fit your disguise. Here are lots of different expressions for you to try.

Secretive   *Giggly*   *Waiting*   *Smug*

Cunning   *Angelic*   *Shy*   *Daft*   *Cool*   *Tired*   *Ill*

Mischievous   *Thinking...*   *Thinking...*   *Thinking...*   *Thinking...*   *...Idea!*

Confused   *Grumpy*   *Anxious*   *Mean*   *Annoyed*   *Surprised*   *Threatening*

Pained   *Doubtful*   *Glum*   *Stern...*   *Sterner...*   *...Sternest*

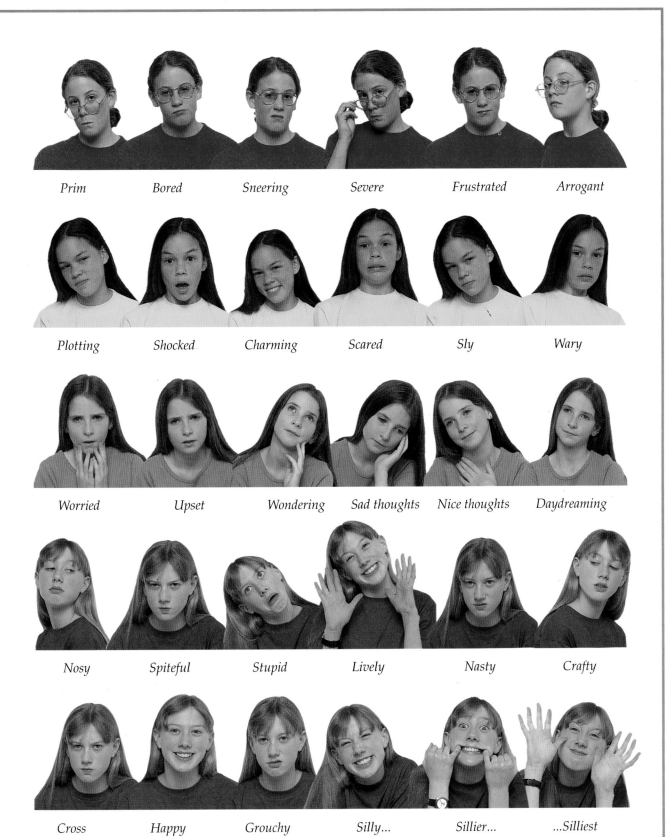

Prim	*Bored*	*Sneering*	*Severe*	*Frustrated*	*Arrogant*
Plotting	*Shocked*	*Charming*	*Scared*	*Sly*	*Wary*
Worried	*Upset*	*Wondering*	*Sad thoughts*	*Nice thoughts*	*Daydreaming*
Nosy	*Spiteful*	*Stupid*	*Lively*	*Nasty*	*Crafty*
Cross	*Happy*	*Grouchy*	*Silly...*	*Sillier...*	*...Silliest*

Disguising your body

Your disguise will be even more effective if you can change the shape of your body and alter the way you move and make gestures.

You will need, to change your shape: small towels; cushion; safety pins; coat. **To change your walk:** ruler; strip of material; pebble.

Ways to change shape

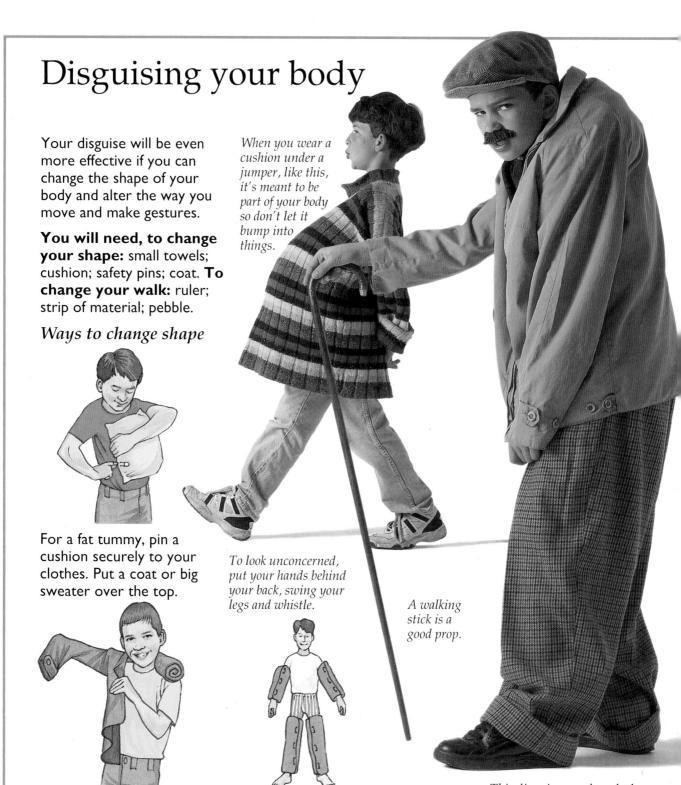

When you wear a cushion under a jumper, like this, it's meant to be part of your body so don't let it bump into things.

For a fat tummy, pin a cushion securely to your clothes. Put a coat or big sweater over the top.

To look unconcerned, put your hands behind your back, swing your legs and whistle.

A walking stick is a good prop.

To make a hunched back, roll up a towel and lay it along your shoulders. Put a jacket on over the top and do it up.

To look bigger, wrap towels around your legs and arms. Safety pin each towel to itself to keep it in place. Wear big clothes on top.

This disguise uses hunched shoulders and leg and arm padding. To look old, walk slowly, taking small steps.

28

In a sporty disguise like this, you might take big steps and swing your arms.

To create a shuffling, painful walk for a tramp disguise like this, try the pebble in the shoe trick, below.

Different walks

The pebble is there to remind you which foot 'hurts'.

For a realistic limp, slip a small pebble in one shoe and pretend that foot really hurts. Try walking like this.

Keep the leg with the ruler on it really straight and try to walk.

For a stiff walk, tie a ruler behind one knee with fabric or a scarf. Hide the ruler under trousers or a long skirt.

Body language

The way you move your head, body and arms, and how you sit, stand and gesture say a lot about the kind of person you are and the mood you are in. This is called body language. The trick of a good disguise is to change your body language to suit the disguise you are in. Watch people closely and try to copy some of their gestures.

Here are some examples.

This person looks eager or nervous. She's sitting on the edge of her seat and clasping her fingers.

Crossed arms and legs and a hanging head make this person look sad or depressed.

This is a relaxed, confident pose. The person is sprawled comfortably in a chair.

Changing your voice

Another way to disguise yourself is to change your voice. Some of the disguises here will only work if you are speaking on a telephone because you look a little bit silly doing them. Make a call to a very good friend and try one of these disguises to see if you can fool them. Or, you could record your voice disguises on a cassette recorder. Play them back to yourself and listen carefully to see if they sound convincing.

You will need: a piece of cloth; a pencil; a telephone or a cassette recorder.

Put the tip of your tongue behind your bottom teeth and try to talk. You won't be able to say 's' properly.

Try to imitate accents that you hear. Listen to them carefully and use a different one for each of your disguises.

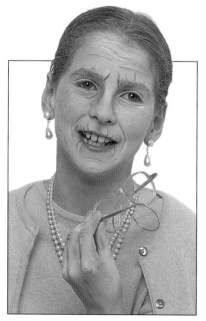

Try speaking very slowly or quickly. Many old people speak slowly. Try speaking very loudly or whispering, too.

Try to talk without moving your mouth. Open it a little and freeze. Speak slowly and as clearly as you can.

Try to make your voice very low or very high. If you disguise youself as a man speak in a deep voice.

Disguises for a telephone or recording

Squeeze your nostrils together as you speak, then try to imitate the sound you make without holding your nose.

Use a piece of cloth to cover the receiver before you speak into it. Ask your friend if your voice sounds different.

Make a shape with your mouth as though you are whistling. Hold this shape and then try to talk.

Hold a pencil sideways between your front teeth. Try to speak clearly, but without letting the pencil fall.

Put a clean finger in one side of your mouth and try talking. Move your finger to another place. Does your voice change?

Make a shape with your mouth as though you are yawning. Keep your mouth like this and try to speak.

Face painting tips

Before you use face paints to disguise your features and hands, make sure your face and hands are clean and completely dry. Put on the clothes you are going to wear for your disguise then lay a small towel around your shoulders. Tuck the towel in around your neck and this will protect your clothes. Take time and care to apply your face paint well as this will make your disguise even more convincing.

Apply your face paint in a bright place. Sit near a window or put a light on either side of your mirror. If you have long hair tie it back or wear a band.

Wash off make-up and water-based face paints with soap and water.

If you are using face paints which are not water-based put a layer of face cream on first. This makes it easier to get the face paint off.

Making foundation from face paint

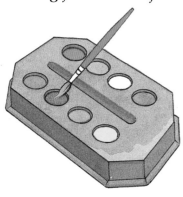

1. Dip your brush in some water, let it drip a little then dabble it in red or brown face paint, depending on the tone of your skin.

2. Brush the face paint onto the back of a margarine tub. Clean your brush, dip it in water then dabble it in white face paint.

Mix enough for your whole face at one time. It's hard to make a new batch match.

You may need to add a little yellow too.

3. Mix some white into the paint until it most nearly matches your skin. You might not need very much white so just mix in a little at a time.

First published in 1996 by Usborne Publishing Ltd, Usborne House, 83-85 Saffron Hill, London EC1N 8RT, England.
Copyright © 1996 Usborne Publishing Ltd. The name Usborne and the device ♛ are Trade marks of Usborne Publishing Ltd. All rights reserved.